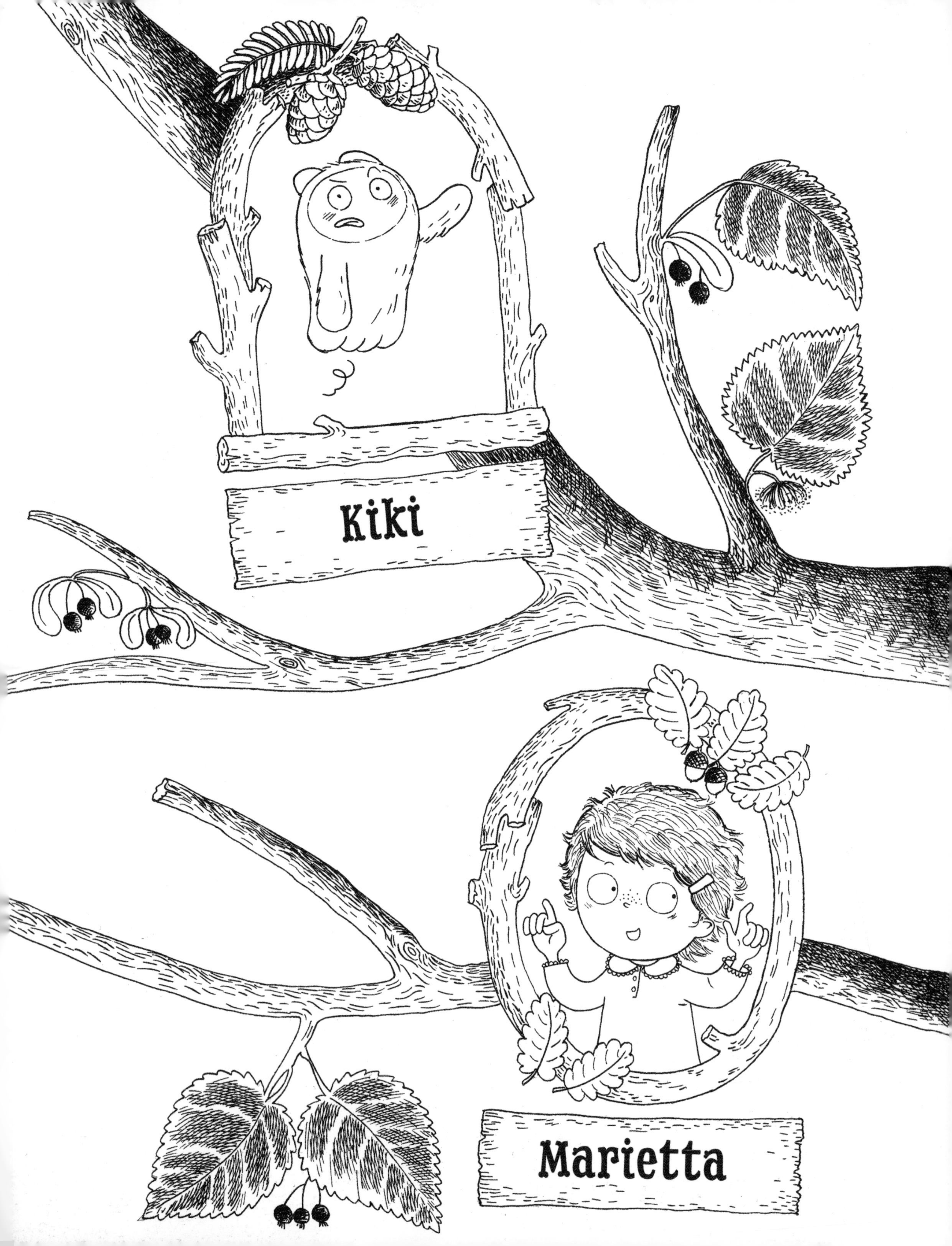
Kiki
Marietta

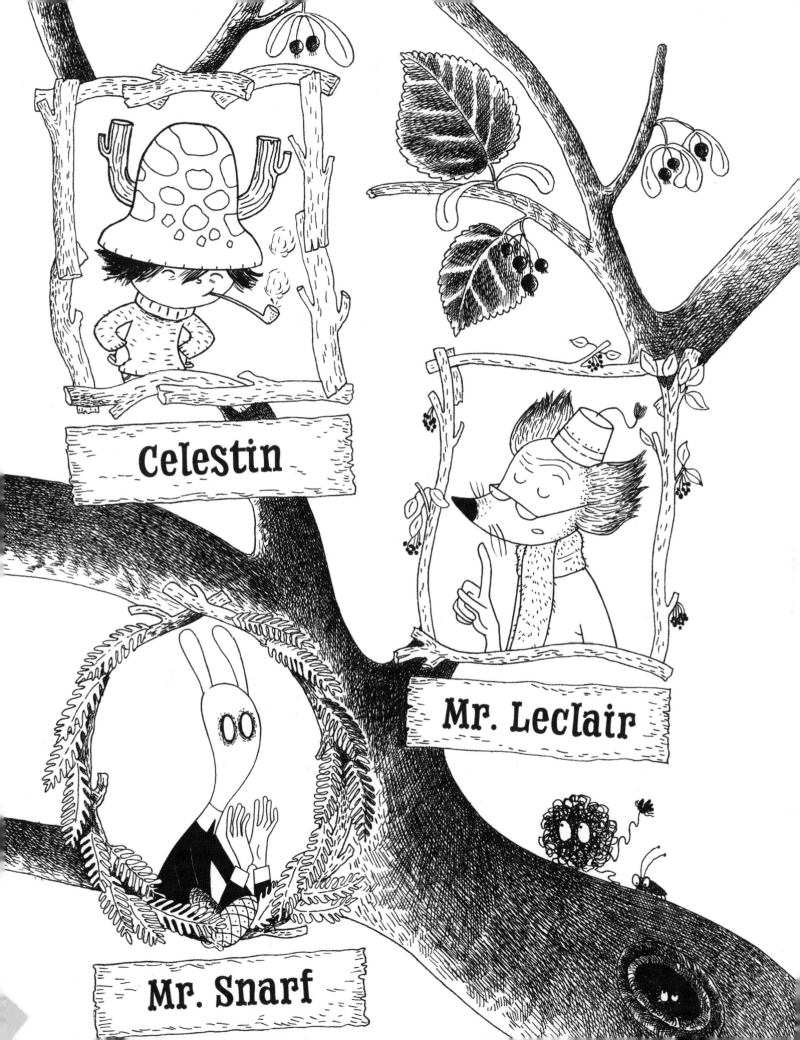

Celestin

Mr. Leclair

Mr. Snarf

HOTEL STRANGE

#3

His Royal Majesty of the Mushrooms

Florian and Katherine Ferrier
illustrations and coloring by Katherine Ferrier

Graphic Universe™ • Minneapolis

Story by Florian and Katherine Ferrier
Illustrations and coloring by Katherine Ferrier
Translation by Carol Klio Burrell

First American edition published in 2016 by Graphic Universe™

Graphic Universe™
A division of Lerner Publishing Group, Inc.
241 First Avenue North
Minneapolis, MN 55401 USA

For reading levels and more information, look up this title at www.lernerbooks.com.

Main body text set in Andy Std Bold 12.5/13.5. Typeface provided by Monotype.

Library of Congress Cataloging-in-Publication Data

The Cataloging-in-Publication Data for *His Royal Majesty of the Mushrooms* is on file at the Library of Congress.
ISBN 978-1-4677-8586-0 (lib. bdg.)
ISBN 978-1-5124-1154-6 (pbk.)
ISBN 978-1-5124-0902-4 (EB pdf)

Manufactured in the United States of America
1 – VP – 7/15/16

It's autumn at Hotel Strange...

And autumn...

...is jam season.

Uh-oh, Marietta! We need more blackberries.

I'm too busy.

KIKI?

3

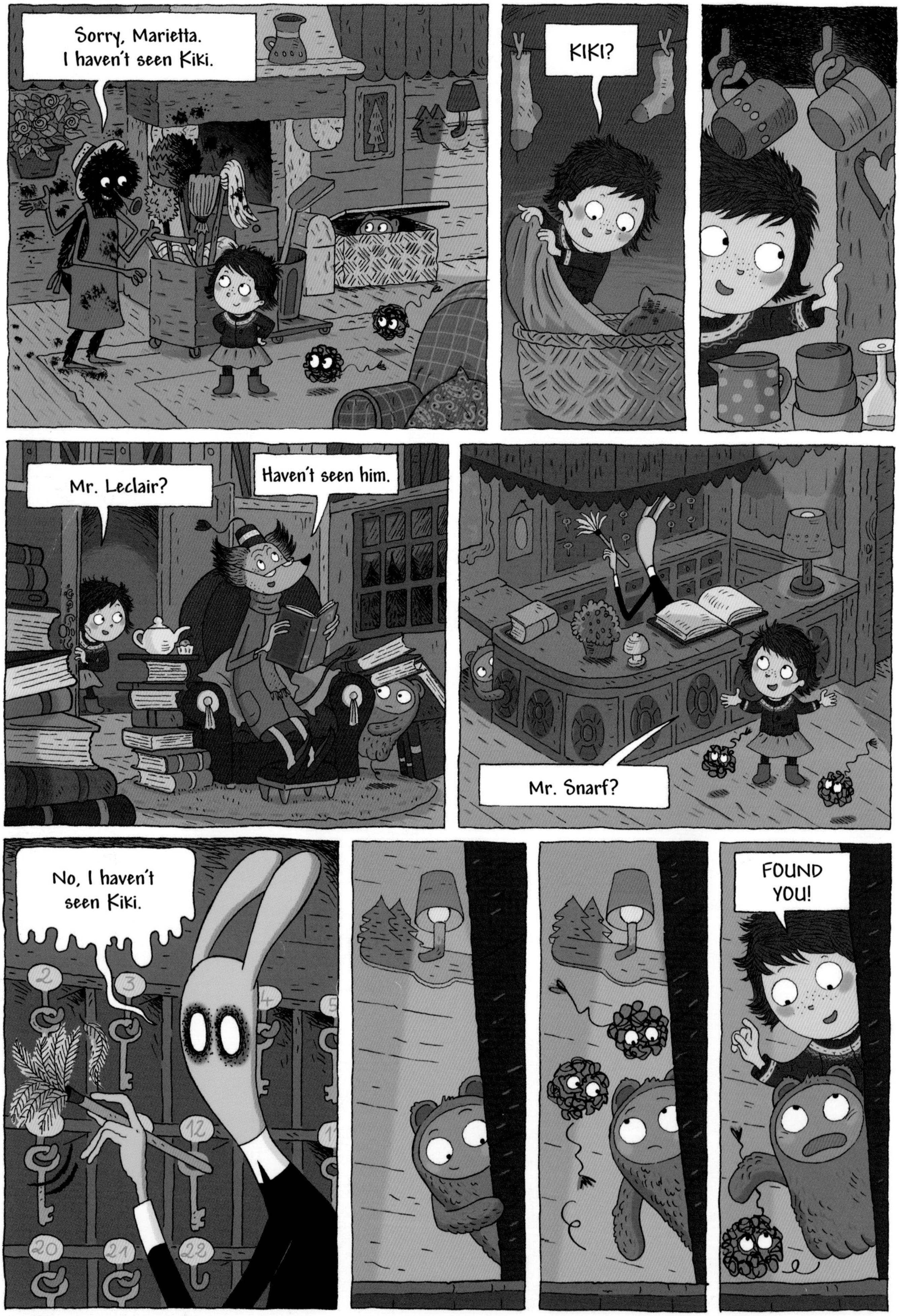
Sorry, Marietta. I haven't seen Kiki.
KIKI?
Mr. Leclair?
Haven't seen him.
Mr. Snarf?
No, I haven't seen Kiki.
2
3
4
5
12
20
21
22
FOUND YOU!

Why do I have to go?

Don't fuss! It's just a little water.

Blackberries are no fun!

5

There he is!

Found him!

It's the KING!

LONG LIVE THE KING!

Um...you've made a mistake.

LONG LIVE THE KING!

Go away, mushrooms!

Come back!

Yep, I'm the King all right!

At your service, Your Majesty!

How may we serve you, Your Majesty?

Um...one or two things...

Nothing huge.

Put everything in the kitchen.

YES, YOUR MAJESTY.

LONG LIVE THE KING!

KIKI?

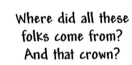

Where did all these folks come from? And that crown?

When you speak to His Highness, you should say: YOUR MAJESTY!

You've made a mistake. Kiki isn't a king.

What's going on?

His Highness has the scepter and the crown...

That makes him our king!

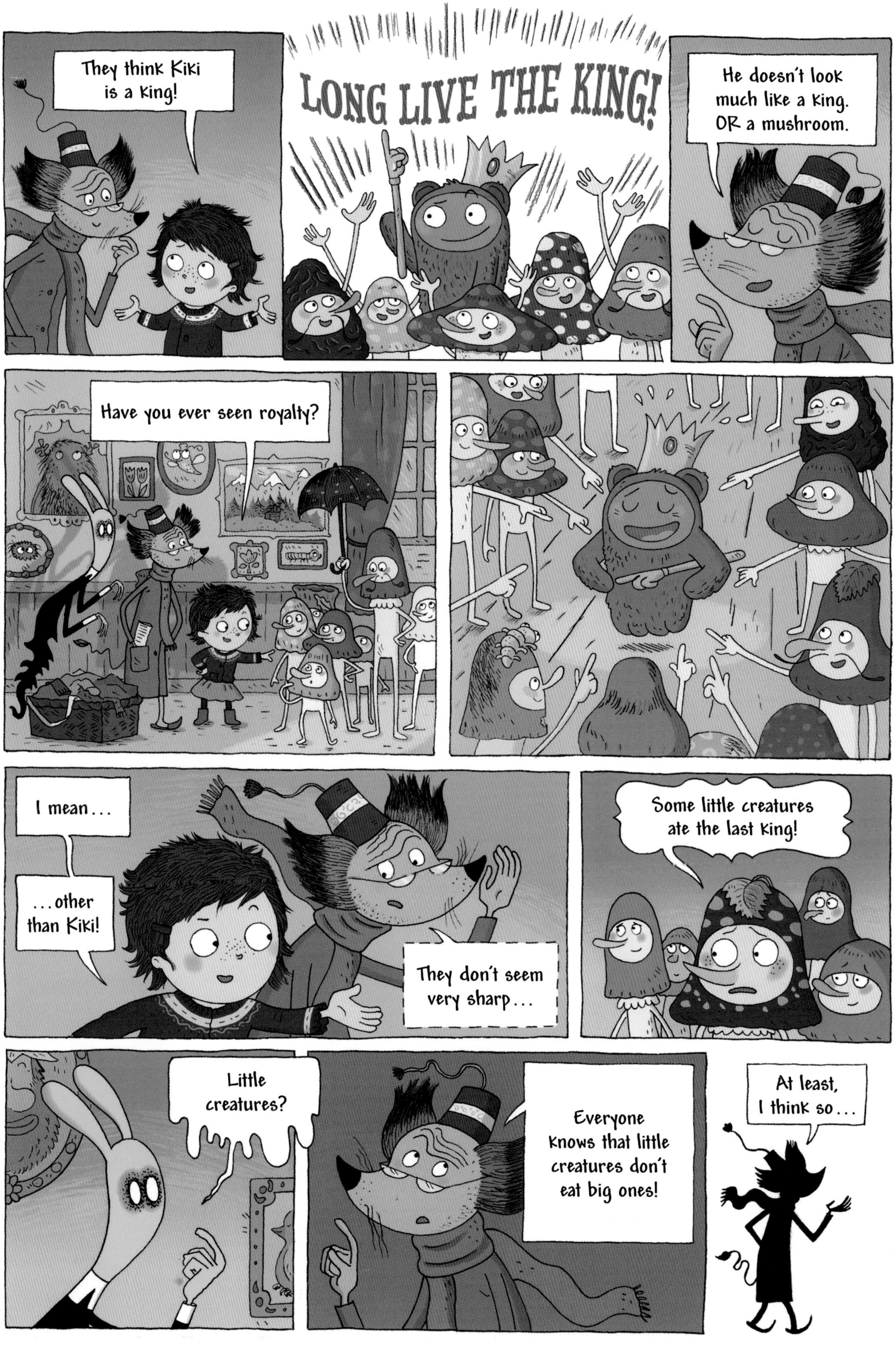
They think Kiki is a king!
LONG LIVE THE KING!
He doesn't look much like a king. OR a mushroom.
Have you ever seen royalty?
I mean...
...other than Kiki!
They don't seem very sharp...
Some little creatures ate the last king!
Little creatures?
Everyone knows that little creatures don't eat big ones!
At least, I think so...

And what if I like being king?

LONG LIVE THE KING!

All right, do what you want.

As long as you do your share.

Here, Kiki... Your... um... Most Highness. It's the list of chores.

Do you need help, Your Greatness?

Why, certainly!

How would you like to be my head general, Mr. Leclair?

They're going to drive me nuts!!

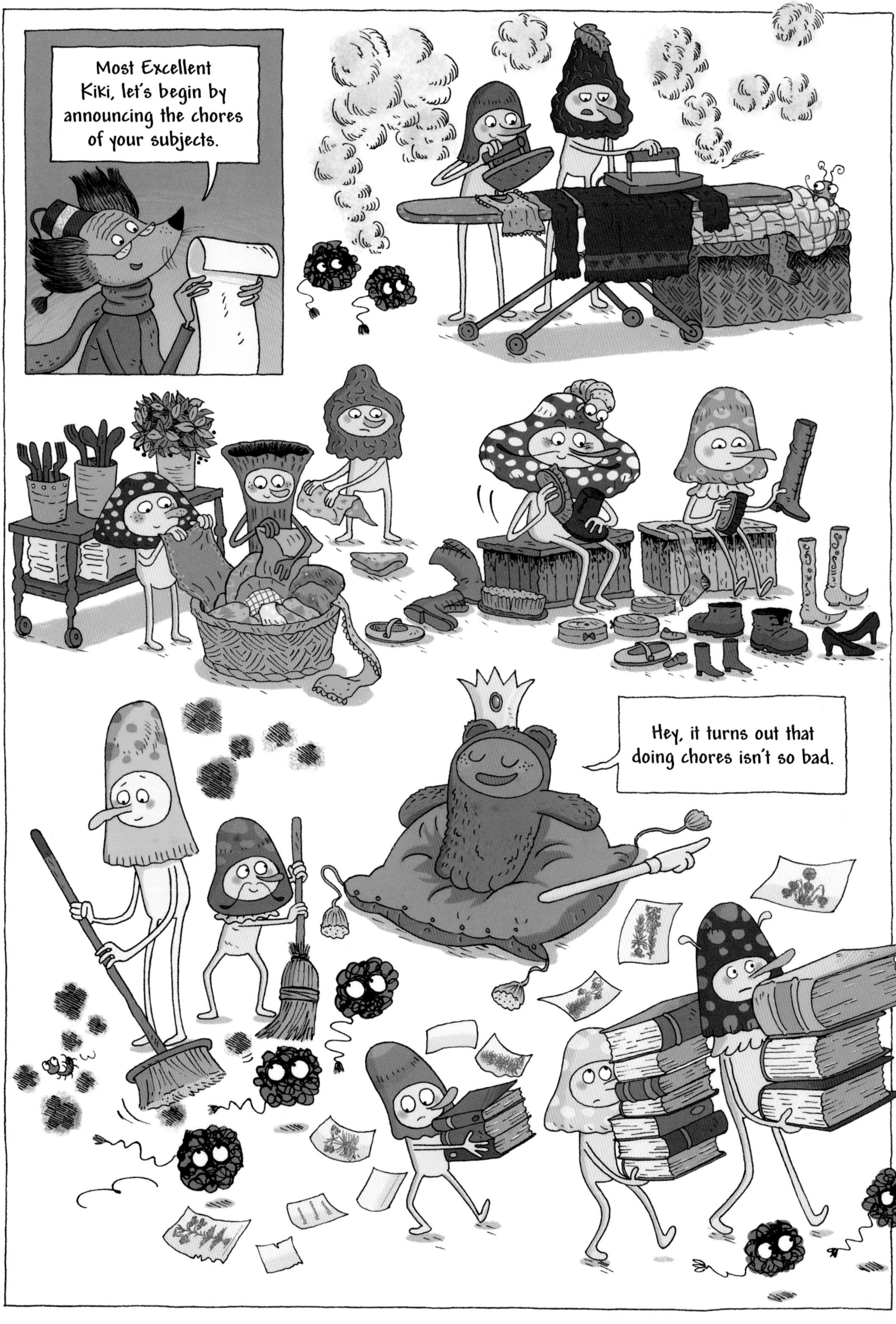
Most Excellent Kiki, let's begin by announcing the chores of your subjects.
Hey, it turns out that doing chores isn't so bad.

I'm worn out, General Leclair. All this work makes me hungry.

We should create an official royal cake!

LONG LIVE THE ROYAL CAKE!

LONG LIVE THE KING!

All right, what have we got?

Other than blackberry jam...

We have some hazelnut fondant.*

Please enjoy...

LONG LIVE THE KING!

12

*A recipe for hazelnut fondant cake is at the end of the book.

The next day...

LONG LIVE THE KING!

LONG LIVE THE KING!

LONG LIVE THE KING!

LONG LIVE THE KING!

LONG LIVE THE KING!

KEEP IT DOWN OUT THERE!

His Excellency is an early bird.

13

Last night, I put the final touches on your speech.

I'll read you the beginning:

"My dear subjects, the new King is called to reign."

Two Rain? What a funny name!

How about Three Snow?

...or One Sun?

Ha, ha. That's enough! You're making fun of me.

Can I just eat my breakfast?

Later, Your Most Serene Highness.

We have to compose your national anthem...

Practice your parading...

And—oh yes! And paint your portrait.

LONG LIVE THE KING!

14

Come in, Your Magnificence.

Have a seat, King Kiki.

Is this going to take long?

No, only a few weeks.

LONG LIVE THE KING!

Long life to the KING!

LONG LIVE THE KING!

LONG LIVE THE KING

LONG LIVE OUR KING
LOOOOONG LIVE THE KIIIIIING
HURRAH FOR THE KING

Have you seen His Highness?

Is there a problem, Mr. Leclair?

Nothing I can't handle.

Your Greatness!

MAJESTY!

MAJESTY!

YOUR MAJESTY!

Nothing's gone right since this crown turned up.

Kiki!

Are they gone?

Sigh. Kiki, don't you think this has gone on long enough?

You're right! I'll give them back the crown.

Here! Being King is no fun!

But, Your Majesty, I'm here to tell you about your palace!

A palace?

I guess I can keep this a little while longer.

SIGH...

17

Hold on, Mr. Leclair!

Aren't you embarrassed to be part of this game?

Come on, Marietta. We're just having fun!

Also, I've always dreamed of being someone important.

General Leclair! We're all waiting for you!

Coming, Your Sparkling Splendidness!

On the way to the palace...

BAM
BAM
BAM

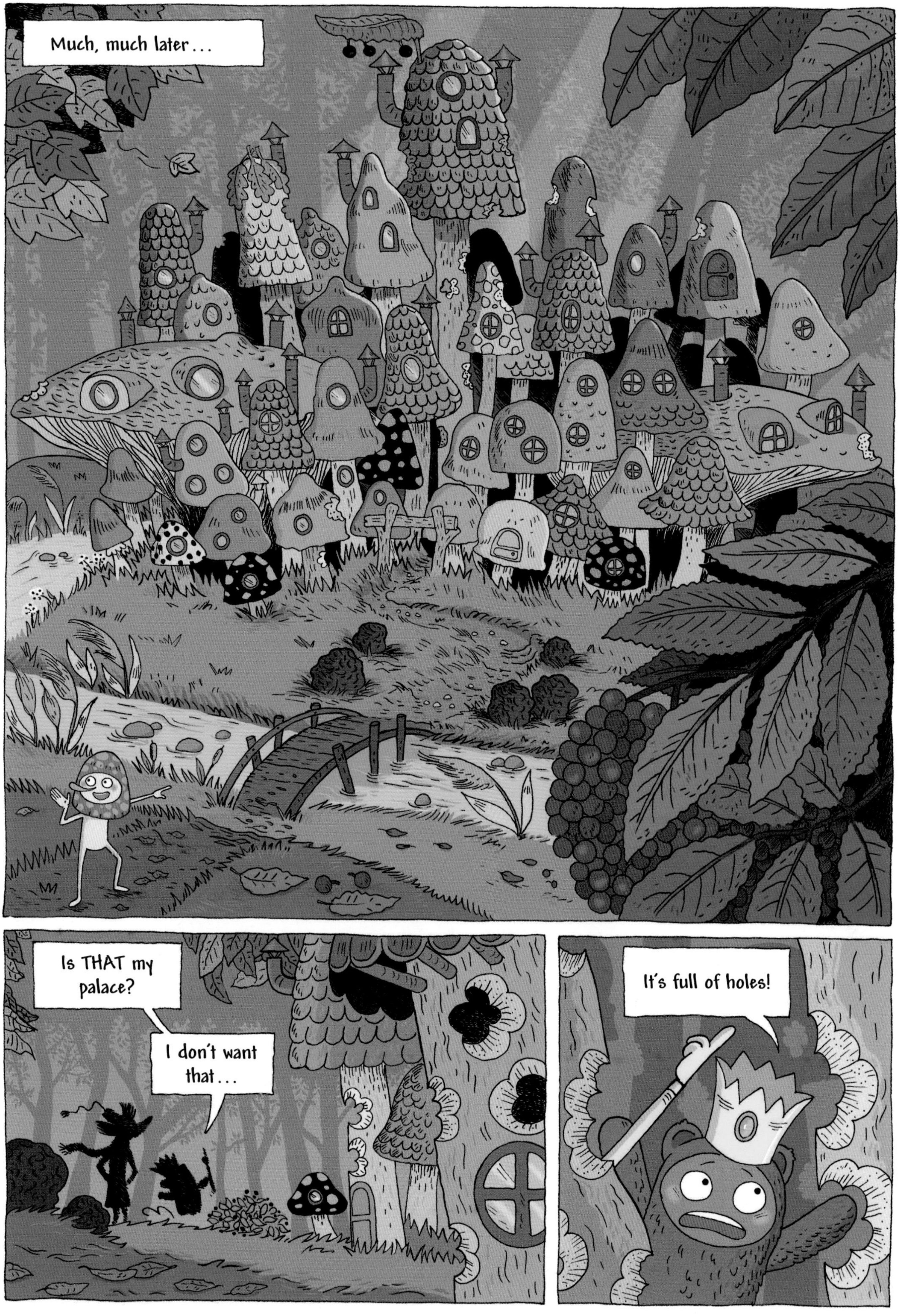

Much, much later...
Is THAT my palace?
I don't want that...
It's full of holes!

Alas, it is, Your Majesty!

We're counting on you...

...to chase away the little creatures...

...who are destroying our village!

KSSSSSS
KSSSSSSS

Those are CROCO-MITES.

Watch out, Your Splendidness!

Aw, these guys are teeny tiny!

What's your advice, my general?

Run away, Majesty!

A little later...

So, how was the palace?

OWW!
Get it off me!

Catch it before it eats everything!

Got it!

WHEW! Nice work!

Uhhhh...

Well...

Croco-mites are big snackers! We're lucky there's only one!

What? Hundreds?

Yes...

More or less...

Do you know what will happen when all those croco-mites get here?

They'll chomp the hotel to bits!

I have an idea!

Let's build a new hotel, someplace nice and warm!

Leave our home? You can't be serious!

This is all because of those stupid mushrooms!

You need to figure out what to do!

Ummmm... maybe we can ask Celestin for advice?

23

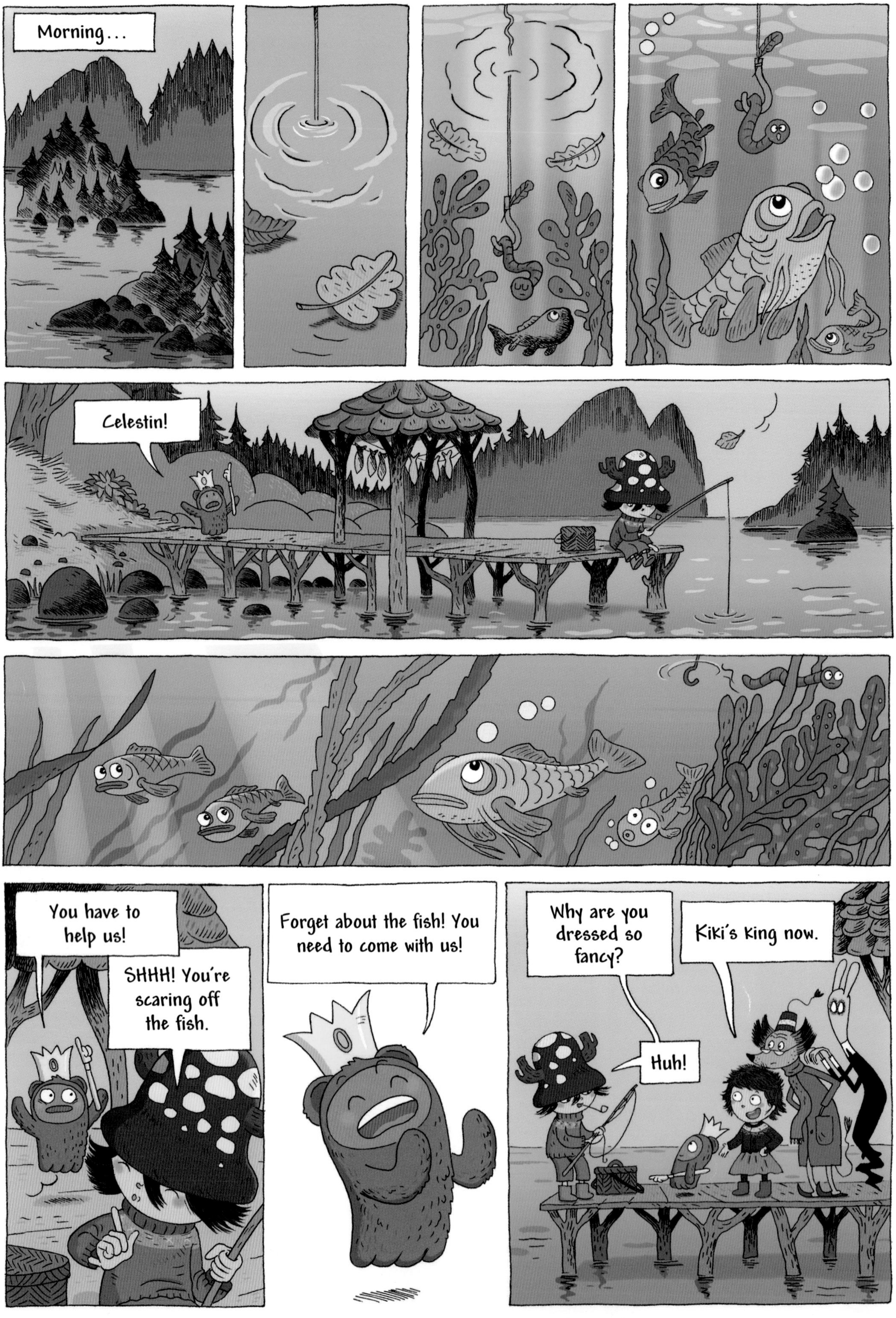
Morning...
Celestin!
You have to help us!
SHHH! You're scaring off the fish.
Forget about the fish! You need to come with us!
Why are you dressed so fancy?
Kiki's king now.
Huh!

Could we change the subject, please?

Croco-mites are eating a village!

Croco-mites? That's no surprise. They eat only wood.

They love it!

They ate my house once.

Then they went away.

That's the solution!

Let them eat the palace.

You can say that because it isn't your home!

What did you do after that, Celestin?

Uh... well...

I built a new house.

The next day...

There are three things you need to know about croco-mites.

One: they bite hard.

Two: they don't like water.

Is this what it's like every morning?

Sigh. Yes!

What's thing number three?

I forgot.

What we need is a plan.

We've brought all the mittens from the attic.

And I have my oven mitts.

Soup's on!

Help yourself!

I found an old general's hat!

BRUSH
BRUSH

Excuse me, Mr. Leclair. What use is a hat?

None. But I look good in it!

Is everybody ready?

The gloves are to catch them. The pots are to hold them.

LONG LIVE HIS MAJESTY!

LONG LIVE THE KING!

We should wait for dawn. It's not polite to disturb people in the middle of the night.

True. But...

...if they're waiting for us, we have nothing to lose!

Now, try not to hurt them.

We won't hurt them. We'll...

SQUASH THEM!

YAAAAAAAAAAAA

28

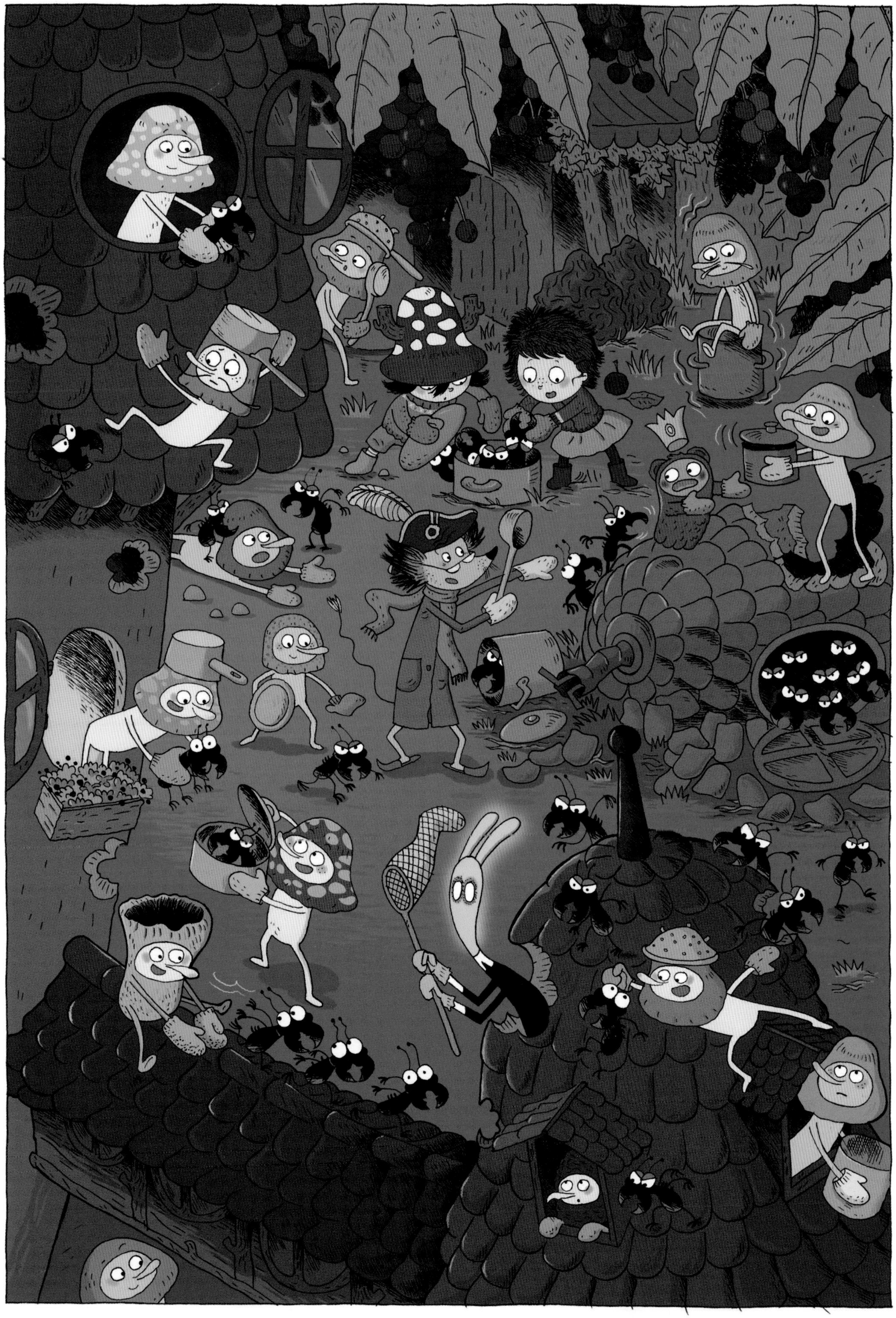

All done, Your Majesty!

That wasn't so hard!

UMMMM...

They're escaping!

Ksss Ksss sss

Ksss

What are you waiting for? Re-catch them!

How odd...I wonder what they're doing.

Oh, now I remember! That's thing number three.

They stick together and become a CROCO-MONSTER!

How did you forget something like that!?

31

Run to the cliff!

The cliff?

But I don't like water either!

Thing number two!

AAAAAH

PLOOP

Water. Ugh!

It's a bit chilly for a swim.

Majesty?

Is it really you?

Golly!

Who's that guy?

That must be the Mushroom King!

The real one!

I thought he got eaten!

I'm so happy to see you again!

Well! Looks like you've upset the croco-mites!

Wait for me here.
I've got this.

The croco-mites are asleep.

No more monster.

Thanks to this sleeping powder from my cousin, the King of the Toadstools.

I left to go find him.

The powder works like a charm on croco-mites.

And it's perfectly safe.

So, you're saying that nobody ate you?

Of course not! Who told you such a silly story?

What do we do with the croco-mites?

I have an idea...

35

They'll be happy on this deserted island.

And they'll have plenty of wood to eat.

I'm just happy to know they'll be far away!

LOOK OUT! THEY'RE WAKING UP!

Ha ha ha! Just kidding!

Morning...

All done!

The croco-mites won't be snacking on my palace again!

You mean THEIR palace, Kiki!

How funny! I have the same crown.

YOU don't have anything on your head but a snail!

I think he's a little crazy.

HO HO HO!
HO HO!
HO HO HO!

Silly me.

This must have fallen off during my trip.

I think you need to give it back...

It'd get heavy after a while.

Next time, take better care of your things.

LONG LIVE THE KING! LONG LIVE THE KING!

Thank you for taking care of my subjects, Kiki.

That was very kind of you.

Your Majesty, do you need a general, by any chance?

Ha ha! No need. We're a peaceful people.

We should get home. There's still a lot to do before winter comes.

Back home at Hotel Strange...

Where did he go now?

Kiki?

Would His Majesty like to help hang the laundry?

Laundry is no fun!

Anyway, I'm not King anymore!

You'll always be a King to us.

King of the sleepyheads!

END

Hazelnut Fondant Cake

Ask an adult for help in the kitchen.

1 cup ground hazelnuts or hazelnut flour
1 cup brown sugar
5 eggs
1 teaspoon (or more) cinnamon, cardamom, or vanilla
butter for coating the pan

1. Preheat oven to 400°F.
2. Mix the hazelnuts, the brown sugar, and the eggs in a mixing bowl.
3. Mix in your choice of cinnamon, cardamom, or vanilla.
4. Pour the batter into a well-buttered tart pan or a silicone baking dish.
5. Ask a grown-up to put the pan or dish inside the oven. Bake for 25 to 30 minutes.
6. Remove cake and let cool for 1 to 2 minutes before serving.

This dessert tastes good either warm and fresh from the oven or the next day, served either plain or with jam. Blackberry jam, for example...

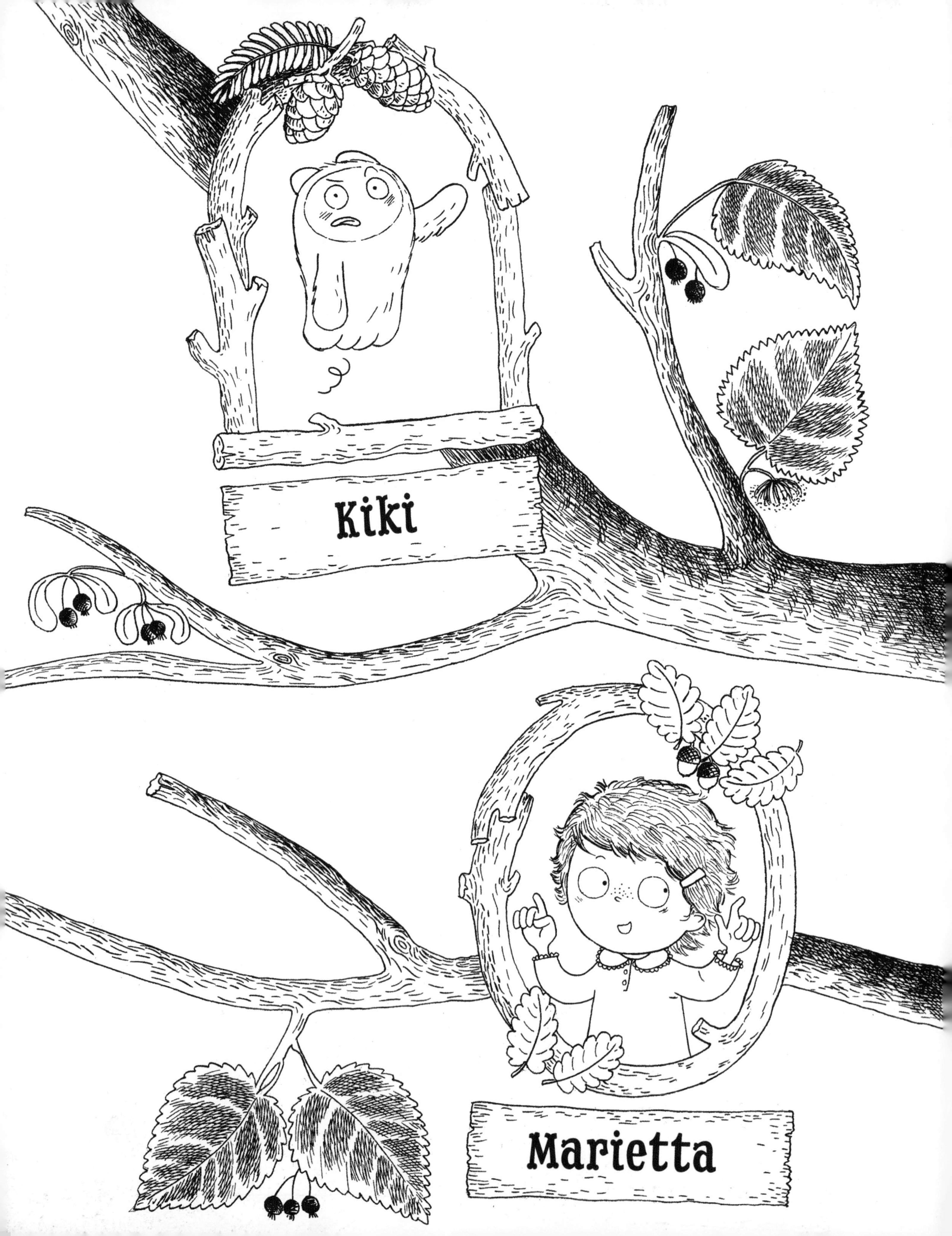
Kiki
Marietta

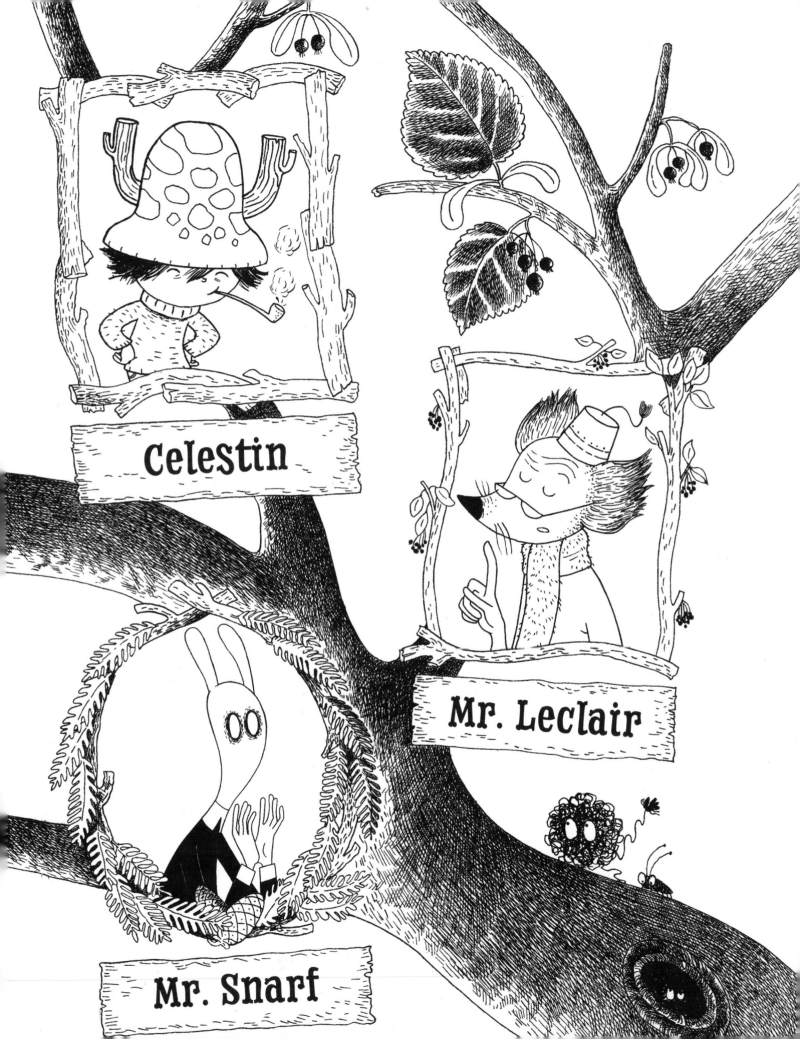

Celestin

Mr. Leclair

Mr. Snarf